Acknowledgments:
Models made by Whoopee! Productions Limited
Illustrations by Martin Aitchison

British Library Cataloguing in Publication Data

Hately, David
    Rupert and the old hat.
    I. Title
    823´.914 [J]
    ISBN 0-7214-1218-1

First edition

Published by Ladybird Books Ltd Loughborough Leicestershire UK
Ladybird Books Inc Auburn Maine 04210 USA

Printed in England

RUPERT
and the
Old Hat

Based on an original story
by Alfred Bestall MBE
Adapted by David Hately

Ladybird Books

One day, Rupert Bear was walking home across the moors. As he neared Nutwood, he found himself surrounded by a thick swirling patch of mist. Soon Rupert couldn't see where he was going.

"**I** hope I'm on the right path," he said as he crossed a ploughed field.

Suddenly, a figure appeared in the mist.

"Oh please!" cried the little bear. "Is this the way to Nutwood village?"

"Hello, Rupert," answered a squeaky voice.

Rupert recognised his friend at once.
The voice belonged to Odmedod,
the scarecrow. He lived in
a field near Nutwood, so
Rupert knew that he was
almost home.

Odmedod was very pleased to see Rupert. "I get so lonely here by myself," he explained. "I wish some of the birds would come to see me, but my job is to scare them away." He sighed, and flopped down to rest.

The two friends sat chatting together for a while and gradually the mist began to clear. Odmedod jumped up with a squeak of alarm.

"**Y**ou'll have to go now, Rupert," he said. "I mustn't be caught sitting down on the job."

So Rupert hurried home, wishing that he could help his lonely friend.

As he walked up the garden path, Rupert noticed that the Nutwood birds were behaving very strangely. They darted about in all directions, chirruping at the top of their voices.

"They all sound so angry," thought Rupert. "I wonder why?"

But when he got indoors he soon forgot about the lonely scarecrow and the angry birds.

Mrs Bear was sorting out some clothes for the scouts' jumble sale. ''Come and help me,'' she called.

"**L**ook at this!" chuckled Mrs Bear as she tried on an old hat. "Don't I look funny? This was once my smartest hat!"

Just then Mr Bear came in from his work in the garden.

"Goodness, I'm hungry," he said. "I'm glad it's lunchtime."

"**I**t can't be twelve o'clock already!" cried Mrs Bear, rushing into the kitchen. "I didn't hear the cuckoo clock."

Mr Bear checked his watch. "It's ten past twelve," he announced.

But Rupert hadn't heard the cuckoo clock either, so he went to see if it had stopped.

"That's odd," thought Rupert as he gazed up at the clock. "That *is* the right time. I wonder if the cuckoo is stuck inside the clock."

But when Rupert opened the little door, he got a surprise. The clock was empty and the cuckoo was nowhere to be seen.

Rupert wandered out into the garden, feeling very puzzled.

Outside, the birds were still making a terrible noise. They seemed to be flying round and round one particular bush, chattering angrily.

Rupert went to have a closer look, but the birds flew away as he came near. In the silence Rupert heard a frightened voice.

"**C**uckoo!" it sobbed. "Cuck…oo!"
And there, clinging to a branch,
was the clock cuckoo.

"Oh, I'm so glad you
came!" cried the
clock cuckoo.
"It's such a long
time since I did
any flying. I just
couldn't go any
further."

Rupert gently picked up the little bird. "Why ever did you leave the clock?" he asked.

"I heard two sparrows talking about my cousin," answered the clock cuckoo. "He's a real cuckoo, not a wooden one like me. He's coming to Nutwood soon with his wife. They spend the summer here, but this year the Nutwood birds are going to drive them away."

"**W**hy?" asked Rupert.

"Because my cousin and his wife put their eggs into other birds' nests to hatch out. The Nutwood birds say they won't put up with it any longer," replied the cuckoo. "I must warn them."

Rupert carried the clock cuckoo indoors and placed him on the windowsill.

"I've had an idea," said Rupert. "You stay here and watch for your cousin. I won't be away for long."

Rupert ran as fast as he could to Odmedod's ploughed field.

"**W**ould you like some guests to keep you company all summer?" asked Rupert.

"That would be lovely!" replied the scarecrow, his eyes shining.

"Then I may be able to help," said Rupert.

He waved goodbye and set off home again.

"**M**ummy!" called Rupert when he reached the house. "May I have that old hat you were going to give to the jumble sale?"

"Of course," said Mrs Bear. "But I can't imagine what you will do with it."

Rupert fetched the old hat and some safety pins.

Suddenly, he heard a frantic call of *Cuckoo! Cuckoo!* from the windowsill.

"My cousin and his wife have just arrived," called the clock cuckoo. "They're hiding in the hedge."

"Don't worry!" said Rupert. "They'll be safe now."

Rupert popped all three cuckoos inside his mummy's hat and took them to meet Odmedod. Then he set to work gathering twigs and bits of straw, which he used to line the old hat. Finally, he pinned the hat inside Odmedod's even older hat and placed it on the scarecrow's head.

"**I**t's a nest!" cried Mrs Cuckoo.
"A lovely, warm nest."

"It's your home for the summer,"
explained Rupert. "Odmedod will make
sure that the other birds don't bother
you, and in return you will keep him
company."

That evening, as Rupert was having his supper, the cuckoo popped out of the clock to tell them all it was seven o'clock.

"Oh, good," said Mrs Bear. "The clock is working again."

Rupert looked up at the clock cuckoo and smiled.

As for the clock cuckoo's cousin and his wife, they had a wonderful summer in Nutwood. None of the other birds dared to try and drive them away, for Odmedod put on his most terrible face to scare them off.

And with all that company, Odmedod could never again complain about feeling lonely!